Contents

1. The Dark Woods   1

2. Leaving Again   10

3. Across the Bridge   17

4. Into the Castle   24

5. Trapped   30

6. Ta-da!   36

7. A Secret Passage   42

8. The Knight   50

9. Under the Moon   56

10. One Mystery Solved   62

CHAPTER ONE

THE DARK WOODS

Jack couldn't sleep.

He put his glasses on. He looked at the clock. It was five-thirty.

Too early to get up.

Yesterday so many strange things had happened. Now he was trying to figure them out.

He turned on the light. He picked up his notebook. He looked at the list he'd made before going to bed.

found tree house in woods

found lots of books in it

pointed to Pteranodon
picture in book

made a wish

went to time of dinosaurs

pointed to a picture of
Frog Creek woods

made a wish

came home to Frog Creek

Jack pushed his glasses into place. Who was going to believe any of this?

His mom wouldn't believe it. Neither would his dad or his third-grade teacher, Ms. Watkins. Only his seven-year-old sister, Annie, understood. She'd gone with him to the time of the dinosaurs.

"Can't you sleep?"

Annie was standing in his doorway.

"Nope," said Jack.

"Me neither," said Annie. "What are you doing?"

She walked over to Jack and looked at his notebook. She read the list.

"Aren't you going to write about the gold medal?" she asked.

"You mean the gold medallion," said Jack.

He picked up his pencil and wrote:

found this in dinosaur time

"Aren't you going to put the letter M on the medal?" said Annie.

"Medallion," said Jack. "Not medal."

He added an M:

"Aren't you going to write about the magic person?" said Annie.

"We don't know for sure if there is a magic person," said Jack.

"Well, someone built the tree house in the woods, and someone put the books in it. Someone lost a gold medal in dinosaur time," said Annie.

"Medallion!" said Jack for the third time. "And I'm just writing the facts. The stuff we know for sure."

"Let's go back to the tree house right now," said Annie, "and find out if the magic person is a fact."

"Are you nuts?" said Jack. "The sun's not even up yet."

"Come on," said Annie. "Maybe we can catch them sleeping."

"I don't think we should go there," said Jack. He was worried. What if the "magic person" was mean? What if he or she didn't want kids to know about the tree house?

"Well, I'm going," said Annie.

Jack looked out his window at the dark gray sky. It was almost dawn.

He sighed. "Okay. Go get dressed. I'll meet you at the back door. Be quiet."

"Yay!" whispered Annie. She tiptoed away as quietly as a mouse.

Jack put on jeans, a warm sweatshirt, and sneakers. He tossed his notebook and pencil in his backpack.

He crept downstairs.

Annie was waiting by the back door. She shined a flashlight in Jack's face. "Ta-da! A magic wand!" she said.

"Shhh! Don't wake up Mom and Dad," whispered Jack. "And turn that flashlight off. We don't want anyone to see us."

Annie nodded and turned the flashlight off. Then she clipped it onto her belt.

Jack and Annie slipped out the door into the cool early-morning air. Crickets were chirping. The dog next door barked.

"Quiet, Henry!" whispered Annie.

Henry stopped barking. Animals always seemed to do what Annie said.

"Let's run!" said Jack.

Jack and Annie dashed across the dark, wet lawn and didn't stop until they reached the Frog Creek woods.

"We need the flashlight now," said Jack.

Annie took it off her belt and switched it on.

Step by step, she and Jack walked between the trees. Jack held his breath. The dark woods were a little scary.

"Gotcha!" said Annie, shining the flashlight in Jack's face.

Jack jumped back. Then he frowned.

"Cut it out!" he said.

"I scared you," said Annie.

Jack glared at her.

"Stop pretending!" he whispered. "This is serious."

"Okay, okay."

Annie shined her flashlight into the tops of the trees.

"Now what are you doing?" said Jack.

"Looking for the tree house!"

The light stopped moving.

The mysterious tree house sat high in the branches of the tallest tree in the woods.

Annie shined her light down the long rope ladder.

"I'm going up," she said. Still holding the flashlight, she began to climb.

"Wait!" Jack called.

What if someone was in the tree house?

"Annie! Come back!"

But Annie was gone. The light had disappeared.

Jack was alone in the dark.

CHAPTER TWO

LEAVING AGAIN

"Annie!" Jack shouted.

"No one's here!" she shouted back.

Jack thought about going home. Then he thought about all the books in the tree house.

He started up the ladder. When he was almost at the top, he saw light in the distant sky. Dawn was starting to break.

Jack crawled through a hole in the tree house floor and took off his backpack.

Annie shined her flashlight on the books scattered about the floor.

"They're still here," she said.

Annie shined the light on a dinosaur book. It was the book that had taken them to the time of dinosaurs.

"Remember the Tyrannosaurus rex?" asked Annie.

Jack shuddered. Of course he remembered! How could anyone forget seeing a real live Tyrannosaurus rex?

The light fell on a book about Pennsylvania. A red silk bookmark stuck out of it.

"Remember the picture of Frog Creek?" said Annie.

"Of course," said Jack. That was the picture that had brought them home.

"There's my favorite," said Annie.

The light was shining on a book about knights and castles. There was a blue leather bookmark in it.

Annie turned to the page with the bookmark.

There was a picture of a knight on a black horse. He was riding toward a castle.

"Annie, close that book," said Jack. "I know what you're thinking."

Annie pointed at the cover.

"Don't, Annie!" said Jack.

"We wish we could go there," Annie said.

"No, we don't!" shouted Jack.

The wind began to moan. The leaves began to tremble.

It was happening again.

"We're leaving!" cried Annie. "Get down!"

The wind moaned louder. The leaves shook harder.

Jack squeezed his eyes shut.

The tree house started to spin.

It spun faster and faster!

Then everything was still.

Absolutely still.

❧ ❧ ❧

Jack opened his eyes. He shivered. The air was damp and cool.

The sound of a horse's whinny came from below.

Neeee-hhhh!

"I think we're here," whispered Annie. She was still holding the castle book.

Jack peeked out the window.

A huge castle loomed out of the fog.

Jack looked around. The tree house was in a different oak tree.

"Look!" said Annie.

Down below, a knight on a black horse was riding by.

"Oh, man," said Jack, "that's incredible. But—we can't stay here. We have to go home and make a plan first." He picked up the book about Pennsylvania. He opened it to the page with the red silk bookmark. He pointed to the photograph of the Frog Creek woods. "I wish—"

"No!" said Annie. She yanked the book away from him. "Let's stay! I want to visit the castle!"

"You're nuts. We need to examine the situation," said Jack. "From home."

"Let's examine it here!" said Annie.

"Come on, Annie." Jack held out his hand. "Give it."

Annie gave Jack the book. "Okay. You can go home. I'm staying," she said. She clipped the flashlight to her belt.

"Wait!" said Jack.

"I'm going to take a peek. A teeny peek," she said. And she scooted down the ladder.

Jack groaned. *Okay, Annie won.* He couldn't leave without her. Besides, he sort of wanted to take a peek himself.

Jack put down the book about Pennsylvania. He dropped the castle book into his pack. He stepped onto the ladder and headed into the cool, misty air.

CHAPTER THREE

ACROSS THE BRIDGE

Annie was under the tree, looking across the foggy ground.

"The knight's riding toward that bridge, I think," said Annie. "The bridge goes to the castle."

"Wait. I'll look it up," said Jack. "Give me the flashlight!"

He took the flashlight from Annie and pulled the castle book out of his pack. He opened it to the page with the leather bookmark.

He read the words under the picture of the knight:

> This is a knight arriving for a castle
> feast. Knights wore armor when
> they traveled long and dangerous
> distances. Armor was very heavy.
> A tournament helmet could weigh up
> to forty pounds.

Wow. Jack had weighed forty pounds when he was five. *It would be like riding a horse with a five-year-old on your head!* he thought.

Jack pulled out his notebook. He wanted to take notes, as he'd done on their dinosaur trip.

He wrote:

heavy head

What else?

He turned the pages of the castle book. He found a picture that showed the whole castle and the buildings around it.

"The knight's crossing the bridge," said Annie. "He's going through the gate. . . . He's gone."

Jack studied the bridge in the picture.

He read:

**A drawbridge crossed the moat.
The moat was filled with water, to
help protect the castle from enemies.
Some people believe crocodiles were
kept in the moat.**

Jack wrote in his notebook:

crocodiles in moat?

"Look!" said Annie, peering through the

mist. "A windmill! Right over there!"

"Yeah, there's a windmill in here, too," said Jack, pointing at the picture.

"Look at the *real* one, Jack," said Annie. "Not the one in the book."

A piercing shriek split the air.

"Yikes," said Annie. "It sounded like it came from that little house over there!" She pointed through the fog.

"There's a little house *here*," said Jack, studying the picture. He turned the page and read:

The hawk house was in the inner ward of the castle. Hawks were trained to hunt other birds and small animals.

Jack wrote in his notebook:

hawks in hawk house

"We must be in the inner ward," said Jack.

"Listen!" whispered Annie. "Do you hear that? Drums! Horns! They're coming from the castle. Let's go see!"

"Wait," said Jack. He turned more pages of the book.

"I want to see what's *really* going on, Jack. Not what's in the book," said Annie.

"But look at this!" said Jack.

He pointed to a picture of a big party. Men were standing by the door, playing drums and horns.

He read:

Feasts were held in the Great Hall. Fanfares were played to announce different dishes in a feast.

"You can look at the book. I'm going to the real feast," said Annie.

"Wait," said Jack, studying the picture. It showed boys his age carrying trays of food. On the trays were peacocks with all their feathers, whole pigs, and pies.

Peacocks? Jack thought.

He wrote:

they eat peacocks?

Jack held up the book to show Annie. "Look, I think they eat—"

Where was she?

Jack looked through the fog.

He heard the real drums and the real horns. He saw the real hawk house, the real windmill, the real moat.

He saw Annie dashing across the real drawbridge. Then she vanished through the gate leading to the castle.

CHAPTER FOUR

INTO THE CASTLE

"Oh, brother," muttered Jack.

He threw his stuff into his pack and moved toward the drawbridge. He hoped no one would see him.

It was getting darker.

When Jack got to the bridge, he started across. The wooden planks creaked under his feet. He peered over the edge of the bridge. *Are there any crocodiles in the moat?* he wondered. He couldn't tell.

"Halt!" someone shouted. A guard on top of the castle wall was looking down.

Jack dashed across the bridge. He ran through the castle gate and into the courtyard. He heard the sounds of music, shouting, and laughter.

Jack hurried to a dark corner and crouched down. He shivered as he looked for Annie.

Torches lit the high wall around the courtyard. The courtyard was nearly empty.

Two boys led horses that clopped over the gray cobblestones. One of them was the knight's black horse.

"Psssst! Jack!"

Jack peered into the darkness.

There was Annie.

She was hiding behind a well in the center of the courtyard. She waved at him.

Jack waved back. He waited until the boys

and horses disappeared inside the stable. Then he dashed to the well.

"I'm going to find the music!" whispered Annie. "Are you coming?"

"Okay," Jack said with a sigh.

They tiptoed together across the cobblestones. Then they slipped through the entrance of the castle.

Laughter and music came from a bright room in front of them. They stood at the doorway and peeked in.

"The feast in the Great Hall!" whispered Jack. He held his breath as he stared in awe.

A giant fireplace blazed at one end of the noisy room. Antlers and rugs hung on the stone walls. Flowers covered the floor.

People in bright clothes and funny hats strolled among the crowd. Some played oddly shaped guitars. Some juggled balls in the air. Some balanced swords on their hands.

Boys in short dresses carried huge trays of food. Dogs were fighting over bones under the tables. Men and women dressed in capes and furs sat at long, crowded wooden tables.

"I wonder which one is the knight," said Jack.

"I don't know," whispered Annie. "But look—they're all eating with their fingers!"

"Halt!" someone shouted behind them.

Jack whirled around.

A man carrying a tray of pies was standing a few feet away.

"Who art thou?" he asked angrily.

"Jack," squeaked Jack.

"Annie," squeaked Annie.

Then they ran as fast as they could down a dimly lit hallway.

CHAPTER FIVE

TRAPPED

"Come on!" cried Annie. "Hurry!"

Jack raced behind her.

"Here! Quick!" Annie dashed toward a door off the hallway. She pushed the door open. Jack and Annie stumbled into a dark, cold room. The door creaked shut behind them.

"Give me the flashlight," said Annie. Jack handed it to her, and she switched it on.

"Yikes!" said Annie. A row of knights was right in front of them!

Annie flicked off the light.

Silence.

"They aren't moving," Jack whispered.

Annie switched the light back on.

"They're just suits," Jack said.

"Without heads," said Annie.

"Let me have the flashlight for a second," said Jack. "So I can look in the book."

Annie handed Jack the flashlight. He pulled out the castle book. He flipped through the pages until he found what he was looking for.

Jack put the book away. "It's called the armory," he said. "It's where armor and weapons are stored."

He shined the flashlight around the room.

"Oh, man," whispered Jack.

The light fell on shiny breastplates, leg plates, and arm plates. Shelves were filled with helmets and weapons. Shields, spears, swords, crossbows, clubs, and battle-axes hung on the walls.

Voices came from the hallway.

"Let's hide!" said Annie.

"Wait," said Jack. "I've got to check on something first."

"Hurry," said Annie.

"It'll take just a second," said Jack. "Hold this." He handed Annie the flashlight.

He tried to lift a helmet from a shelf. It was too heavy.

He bent down and dragged the helmet over his head. The visor slammed shut.

Oh, man, thought Jack. *This is worse than having a five-year-old on my head. It's like having a ten-year-old on my head!*

Not only could Jack not lift his head, he couldn't see anything, either.

"Jack!" Annie sounded far away. "They're getting closer!"

"Turn off the flashlight!" Jack's voice echoed inside the metal helmet.

He struggled to get the helmet off.

Suddenly he lost his balance and went crashing into other pieces of armor. Metal plates and weapons clattered to the floor.

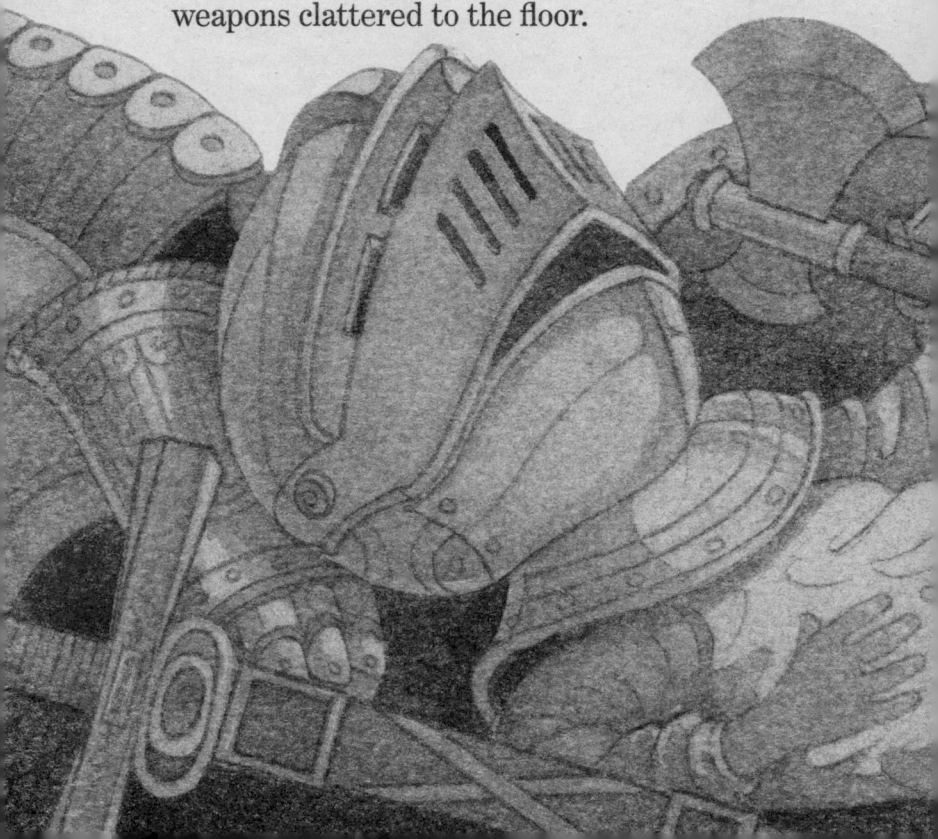

Jack lay on the floor in the dark. He tried to get up. But his head was too heavy.

He heard deep voices.

Someone grabbed him by the arm. The next thing he knew, his helmet was yanked off. He was staring into the fiery light of a torch.

CHAPTER SIX

TA-DA!

In the torchlight, Jack saw three huge men standing over him.

One with very squinty eyes held the torch. One with a very red face held Jack. And one with a very long mustache held on to Annie.

Annie was kicking and yelling.

"Stop!" said the one with the very long mustache.

"Who art thou?" said the one with the very red face.

"Spies? Foreigners? Egyptians? Romans? Persians?" said the squinty-eyed one.

"No, you dummies!" said Annie.

"Oh, brother," Jack muttered.

"Arrest them!" said Red Face.

"The dungeon!" said Squinty Eyes.

The guards marched Jack and Annie out of the armory.

"Go!" said a guard, giving him a push.

Jack went.

Squinty, Annie, Mustache, Jack, and Red marched down the long, dark hallway. They marched down a narrow, winding staircase.

Jack heard Annie shouting at the guards. "Meanies! We didn't do anything!"

The guards laughed.

At the bottom of the stairs was a big iron door with a bar across it. Squinty lifted the bar. He shoved the door, and it creaked open.

Mustache and Red pushed Jack and Annie into a cold, clammy room.

The fiery torch lit the dungeon. There were chains hanging from the filthy walls. Water dripped from the ceiling, making puddles on the stone floor. It was the creepiest place Jack had ever seen.

"We'll keep them here till the feast is done. Then turn them over to the duke," said Squinty. "He knows how to take care of thieves."

"There will be a hanging tomorrow," said Mustache.

"If the rats don't get them first," said Red.

They all laughed.

Jack felt his backpack move. Annie was quietly opening it.

"Come on, let's chain the two of 'em," said Squinty.

The guards started toward Jack and Annie. Annie whipped her flashlight out of Jack's pack.

"Ta-da!" she yelled.

The guards froze. They stared at the shiny flashlight in Annie's hand.

Annie switched on the light. The guards gasped. They jumped back against the wall.

Squinty dropped the torch. It fell into a dirty puddle on the floor, sputtered, and went out.

"My magic wand!" Annie said, waving the flashlight. "Get down. Or I'll wipe you out!"

Jack's mouth dropped open.

Annie fiercely pointed her light at Squinty, then at Mustache, and then at Red. Each howled and covered his face.

"Down! All of you! Get down!" shouted Annie.

One by one, the guards knelt down on the wet floor.

Jack couldn't believe it.

"Come on," Annie whispered to Jack. "Let's go now."

Jack looked at the open doorway. He looked at the guards quaking on the ground.

"Hurry!" said Annie.

In one quick leap, Jack followed Annie out of the terrible dungeon.

CHAPTER SEVEN

A SECRET PASSAGE

Annie and Jack raced back up the winding stairs and down the long hallway.

They hadn't gone far when they heard shouting behind them.

Dogs barked in the distance.

"They're coming!" Annie cried.

"In here!" said Jack. He shoved open a door off the hallway and pulled Annie into a dark room.

Jack pushed the door shut. Then Annie

shined her flashlight around the room. There were rows of sacks and wooden barrels.

"I'd better look in the book," said Jack, pulling out the book and flipping through the pages.

"Shhh!" said Annie. "Someone's coming."

Jack and Annie jumped behind the door as it creaked open.

Jack held his breath. A light from a torch danced wildly over the sacks and barrels.

The light disappeared. The door slammed shut.

"Oh, man," whispered Jack. "We have to hurry. They might come back."

His hands were trembling as he turned the pages of the castle book.

"Here's a map of the castle," he said. "Look, this must be the room we're in. It's a storeroom." Jack studied the room in the book. "These are sacks of flour and barrels of wine."

"Who cares? We have to go!" said Annie. "Before they come back!"

"No. Look," said Jack. He pointed at the map. "There's a trapdoor."

He read aloud:

In this castle, a trapdoor led from the storeroom through a secret passage to a precipice over the moat.

"What's a precipice?" said Annie.

"I don't know. We'll find out," said Jack. "But first we have to find the trapdoor."

Jack looked at the picture carefully. Then he shined the flashlight around the room.

The floor of the room was made of stones. The trapdoor in the picture was five stones from the door to the hallway.

Jack shined the light on the floor and

counted the stones out loud. "One, two, three, four, five."

He stamped on the fifth stone. It was loose!

Jack put the flashlight on the floor. He worked his fingers under the thin slab of stone and tried to lift it.

"Help," Jack said. "It's heavy!"

Annie helped Jack lift the stone square out of its place. Underneath was a small wooden door.

Jack and Annie tugged on the rope handle of the door. The door fell open with a *thunk*.

Jack picked up the flashlight and shined it down the hole.

"There's a little ladder," he said. "Let's go!"

He clipped the flashlight onto his belt and felt his way down the small ladder. Annie followed.

When they reached the bottom of the

ladder, Jack shined the light around them.

There was a tunnel!

Jack crouched down and began moving through the damp, creepy tunnel. The flashlight dimly flickered across the stone walls.

He shook the light. Were the batteries going dead?

"I think our light's dying!" he said to Annie.

"Hurry!" she called from behind him.

Jack went faster. His back hurt from crouching.

The light got dimmer and dimmer. Jack was desperate to get out of the castle before the batteries died completely.

Soon he reached another small wooden door. It was the door at the end of the tunnel!

Jack unlatched the door and pushed it open.

He poked his head outside.

He couldn't see anything in the misty darkness.

The air felt cool and fresh. He took a deep breath.

"Where are we?" whispered Annie behind him. "What do you see?"

"Nothing. But I think we've come to the outside of the castle," said Jack. "I'll find out."

Jack put the flashlight in his pack. He put the pack on his back. He stuck his hand out the door. He couldn't feel the ground. "I'm going to have to go feet first," he said.

Jack turned around in the small tunnel. He lay down on his stomach. He stuck one leg out the door. Then the other.

Jack inched down, bit by bit, until he was hanging out the door, clinging to the ledge.

"This must be the precipice!" he called to Annie. "I can't touch the ground. Pull me up!"

Annie reached for Jack's hands. "I can't hold you!" she said.

Jack felt his fingers slipping. Then down he fell through the darkness.

SPLASH!

CHAPTER EIGHT

THE KNIGHT

Water filled Jack's nose and covered his head. His glasses slipped off. He grabbed them just in time. He coughed and flailed his arms.

"Jack!" Annie was calling from above.

"I'm in . . . the moat!" said Jack, gasping for air. He tried to tread water and put his glasses back on. With his backpack, his shoes, and his heavy clothes, he could barely stay afloat.

SPLASH!

"Hi! I'm here!" Annie sputtered.

Jack could hear Annie nearby, but he couldn't see her.

"Which way's land?" Annie asked.

"I don't know! Just swim!"

Jack dog-paddled through the cold black water.

He heard Annie swimming, too. At first it seemed as if she was swimming in front of him. But then he heard a splash behind him.

"Annie?" he called.

"What?" Her voice came from in front. *Not behind.*

Another splash. *Behind.*

Jack's heart almost stopped. *Crocodiles?* He couldn't see anything through his water-streaked glasses.

"Annie!" he whispered.

"What?"

"Swim faster!"

"But I'm here! I'm over here! Near the edge!" she whispered.

Jack swam through the dark toward her voice. He imagined a crocodile slithering after him.

Jack's hand touched a wet, live thing.

"*Ahhhh!*" he cried.

"It's me! Take my hand!" said Annie.

Jack grabbed her hand. She pulled him to the edge of the moat. They crawled over an embankment onto the wet grass.

"Oh, man," Jack said.

He was shivering all over. His teeth were chattering. He shook the water off his glasses and put them back on.

It was so misty he couldn't see the castle. He couldn't even see the moat, much less a crocodile.

"We . . . we made it," said Annie. Her teeth were chattering, too.

"I know," said Jack. "But where are we?" He peered at the foggy darkness.

Where was the drawbridge? The windmill? The hawk house? The grove of trees? The tree house?

Everything had been swallowed up by the thick, soupy darkness.

Jack reached into his wet backpack and pulled out the flashlight. He pushed the switch. Nothing happened. The batteries were dead.

They were trapped, but not in a dungeon. They were trapped in the still, cold darkness.

Neeee-hhhh!

A horse's whinny echoed through the night.

The clouds parted. A full moon was shining in the sky. A pool of light spread through the mist.

Jack and Annie saw a shadowy figure just a few feet away. It was the knight.

The knight sat on the black horse. His armor shone in the moonlight. A visor hid his face, but he seemed to be staring straight at Jack and Annie.

CHAPTER NINE

UNDER THE MOON

Jack froze.

"It's him," Annie whispered.

The knight held out his gloved hand.

"Come on, Jack," Annie said.

"Where are you going?" said Jack.

"He wants to help us," said Annie.

"How do you know?" said Jack.

"I can just tell," said Annie.

Annie stepped toward the horse. The knight dismounted.

The knight picked Annie up and put her on the back of his horse.

"Come on, Jack," Annie called.

Jack moved slowly toward the knight. The knight lifted him up, too, and put him on the horse, behind Annie.

The knight then got on behind them. He slapped the reins.

The black horse cantered beside the moonlit water of the moat.

Jack rocked back and forth in the saddle. The wind blew his hair. He felt very brave and very powerful.

He felt as if he could ride forever on this horse, with this mysterious knight, over the ocean, over the world, over the moon.

A hawk shrieked in the darkness.

"There's the tree house," said Annie. She pointed toward a grove of trees.

The knight guided the horse toward the trees.

"See. There it is," Annie said, pointing to the ladder.

The knight brought his horse to a stop. He dismounted and helped Annie and Jack down.

"Thank you, sir," Annie said. She bowed.

"Thank you," Jack said. He bowed, too.

The knight got back on his horse. He raised his gloved hand. Then he slapped the reins and rode off through the mist.

Annie started up the tall ladder, and Jack followed. They climbed into the dark tree house and looked out the window.

The knight was riding toward the outer wall of the castle. They saw him go through the outer gate.

Clouds started to cover the moon again. For a brief moment, Jack thought he saw the knight's armor gleaming on the top of a hill beyond the castle.

The clouds covered the moon completely. A black mist swallowed the land.

"He's gone," whispered Annie.

Jack shivered in his wet clothes as he kept staring at the blackness.

"I'm cold," said Annie. "Where's the Pennsylvania book?"

Jack heard Annie fumbling in the darkness. He kept looking out the window.

"I think this is it," said Annie. "I feel a silk bookmark."

Jack was only half-listening. He was hoping to see the knight's armor gleam again in the distance.

"Okay. I'm going to use this," said Annie. "Because I think it's the right one. Here goes. Okay. I'm pointing. I'm going to make a wish. I wish we could go to Frog Creek!"

Jack heard the wind begin to blow softly.

"I hope I pointed to the right picture in the right book," said Annie.

"What?" Jack looked back at her. "Right picture? Right book?"

The tree house began to rock. The wind got louder and louder.

"I hope it wasn't the dinosaur book!" said Annie.

"Stop!" Jack shouted at the tree house.

Too late.

The tree house started to spin.

It spun faster and faster!

Then everything was still.

Absolutely still.

CHAPTER TEN

ONE MYSTERY SOLVED

The air was warm.

It was dawn. Far away a dog barked.

"I think that's Henry barking!" Annie said.

Jack and Annie both looked out the tree house window.

"We're home!" said Annie. "Yay!"

"That was close," said Jack.

In the distance, streetlights glowed near their house. There was a light on in their upstairs window.

"Uh-oh," said Annie. "I think Mom and Dad are up. Hurry!"

"Wait." In a daze, Jack opened his pack. He pulled out the castle book. It was quite wet. But Jack placed it back with all the other books.

"Come on!" said Annie. She started climbing out of the tree house.

Jack followed her down the rope ladder.

They reached the ground and took off running between the gray-black trees.

They left the woods and ran down their quiet street.

They got to their yard and crept across the lawn.

They opened the front door carefully and slipped inside their house.

"They're not downstairs yet," whispered Annie.

"Shhh," said Jack.

He led the way up the stairs and down the hall. There was no sign of their mom or dad, but Jack could hear water running in the bathroom.

Their house was so different from the dark, cold castle. It was safe and cozy and friendly.

Annie stopped at her bedroom door. She gave Jack a smile, then disappeared inside her room.

Jack hurried into his room. He took off his damp clothes and pulled on his dry, soft pajamas.

He sat down on his bed and opened his backpack. He took out his wet notebook. He felt around for the pencil, but his hand touched something else.

Jack pulled the blue leather bookmark out of his pack. It must have fallen out of the castle book.

Jack held the bookmark close to his lamp and studied it. The leather was smooth and worn. It seemed ancient.

For the first time Jack noticed a letter on the bookmark. It was a fancy M.

Jack opened the drawer next to his bed. He took out the gold medallion.

He looked at the letter on it. It was the same M.

Now this *was an amazing new fact.*

Jack took a deep breath. At least that was one mystery solved.

The person who had dropped the gold medallion in the time of the dinosaurs was the same person who owned all the books in the tree house.

Who *was* this person?

Jack placed the bookmark next to the medallion. He closed the drawer.

Jack picked up his pencil. He turned to the least wet page in his notebook and started to write down this new fact.

the same

But before he could draw the M, his eyes closed.

Jack dreamed they were with the knight again. All three of them were riding the black horse through the cool, dark night. They rode beyond the outer wall of the castle and up over a moonlit hill.

Then they all rode into the mist.

Here's a special preview of
Magic Tree House® Fact Tracker

Knights and Castles

After their adventure in the Middle Ages,
Jack and Annie wanted to know more about
knights and castles. Track the facts with them!

Available now!

Lords and Ladies

In the Middle Ages, most rich people were *nobles*. Nobles came from families that had been wealthy for a long time.

Noble women were called *ladies*. They could also have titles, such as baroness, duchess, or countess.

Lady Annie,
Countess of Pennsylvania

Lord Jack,
Duke of Frog Creek

Noble men sometimes had titles such as baron, duke, or count.

The feudal system helped keep order during the Middle Ages. But it wasn't very fair.

A person almost always had to be born into the nobility. Even people who worked very hard and became rich could not normally become nobles.

Today in Europe, America, and many other places around the world, people are free to try to be almost anything they want.

Holiday magic and mystery abound in the beloved classic
CHRISTMAS IN CAMELOT!

Share this newly illustrated deluxe holiday edition with your loved ones and celebrate the magic of the season!

Don't miss

Magic Tree House® #3

MUMMIES IN THE MORNING

Jack and Annie travel to
Egypt and come face to face
with a dead queen. . . .

Available now!

Magic Tree House®

#1: Dinosaurs Before Dark

#2: The Knight at Dawn

#3: Mummies in the Morning

#4: Pirates Past Noon

#5: Night of the Ninjas

#6: Afternoon on the Amazon

#7: Sunset of the Sabertooth

#8: Midnight on the Moon

#9: Dolphins at Daybreak

#10: Ghost Town at Sundown

#11: Lions at Lunchtime

#12: Polar Bears Past Bedtime

#13: Vacation Under the Volcano

#14: Day of the Dragon King

#15: Viking Ships at Sunrise

#16: Hour of the Olympics

#17: Tonight on the *Titanic*

#18: Buffalo Before Breakfast

#19: Tigers at Twilight

#20: Dingoes at Dinnertime

#21: Civil War on Sunday

#22: Revolutionary War on Wednesday

#23: Twister on Tuesday

#24: Earthquake in the Early Morning

#25: Stage Fright on a Summer Night

#26: Good Morning, Gorillas

#27: Thanksgiving on Thursday

#28: High Tide in Hawaii

Magic Tree House® Merlin Missions

#1: Christmas in Camelot

#2: Haunted Castle on Hallows Eve

#3: Summer of the Sea Serpent

#4: Winter of the Ice Wizard

#5: Carnival at Candlelight

#6: Season of the Sandstorms

#7: Night of the New Magicians

#8: Blizzard of the Blue Moon

#9: Dragon of the Red Dawn

#10: Monday with a Mad Genius

#11: Dark Day in the Deep Sea

#12: Eve of the Emperor Penguin

#13: Moonlight on the Magic Flute

#14: A Good Night for Ghosts

#15: Leprechaun in Late Winter

#16: A Ghost Tale for Christmas Time

#17: A Crazy Day with Cobras

#18: Dogs in the Dead of Night

#19: Abe Lincoln at Last!

#20: A Perfect Time for Pandas

#21: Stallion by Starlight

#22: Hurry Up, Houdini!

#23: High Time for Heroes

#24: Soccer on Sunday

#25: Shadow of the Shark

#26: Balto of the Blue Dawn

#27: Night of the Ninth Dragon

Magic Tree House®
Super Edition

#1: World at War, 1944

Magic Tree House®
Fact Trackers

Dinosaurs
Knights and Castles
Mummies and Pyramids
Pirates
Rain Forests
Space
Titanic
Twisters and Other Terrible Storms
Dolphins and Sharks
Ancient Greece and the Olympics
American Revolution
Sabertooths and the Ice Age
Pilgrims
Ancient Rome and Pompeii
Tsunamis and Other Natural Disasters
Polar Bears and the Arctic
Sea Monsters
Penguins and Antarctica
Leonardo da Vinci
Ghosts
Leprechauns and Irish Folklore
Rags and Riches: Kids in the Time of
  Charles Dickens
Snakes and Other Reptiles
Dog Heroes
Abraham Lincoln

Pandas and Other Endangered Species
Horse Heroes
Heroes for All Times
Soccer
Ninjas and Samurai
China: Land of the Emperor's Great
  Wall
Sharks and Other Predators
Vikings
Dogsledding and Extreme Sports
Dragons and Mythical Creatures
World War II

More Magic Tree House®

Games and Puzzles from the Tree House
Magic Tricks from the Tree House
My Magic Tree House Journal
Magic Tree House Survival Guide
Animal Games and Puzzles
Magic Tree House Incredible Fact Book

For Nathaniel Pope

Text copyright © 1993, 2013 by Mary Pope Osborne
Cover art and interior illustrations copyright © 1993, 2013 by Sal Murdocca

All rights reserved. Published in the United States by Random House Children's Books, a division of Penguin Random House LLC, New York. Originally published in paperback and in different form by Random House Children's Books, New York, in 1993. This edition features revised text and art that first appeared in the hardcover edition published by Random House Children's Books, New York, in 2013.

Random House and the colophon are registered trademarks and A Stepping Stone Book and the colophon are trademarks of Penguin Random House LLC. Magic Tree House is a registered trademark of Mary Pope Osborne; used under license.

Visit us on the Web!
SteppingStonesBooks.com | randomhousekids.com | MagicTreeHouse.com

Educators and librarians, for a variety of teaching tools, visit us at
RHTeachersLibrarians.com

Library of Congress Cataloging-in-Publication Data
Osborne, Mary Pope.
The knight at dawn / by Mary Pope Osborne ; illustrated by Sal Murdocca.
p. cm.
(The Magic Tree House) A First Stepping Stone book
Summary: Eight-year-old Jack and his younger sister Annie use the magic tree house to travel back to the Middle Ages, where they explore a castle and are helped by a mysterious knight.
ISBN 978-0-679-82412-1 (trade) — ISBN 978-0-679-92412-8 (lib. bdg.) —
ISBN 978-0-375-89419-0 (ebook)
[1. Time travel—Fiction. 2. Castles—Fiction. 3. Middle Ages—Fiction.
4. Knights and knighthood—Fiction. 5. Magic—Fiction. 6. Tree houses—Fiction.]
I. Murdocca, Sal, ill. II. Title. III. Series: Osborne, Mary Pope. Magic tree house
series ; #2.
PZ7.O81167Kn 1993 [Fic]—dc20 92-13705

Printed in the United States of America 91

This book has been officially leveled by using the F&P Text Level Gradient™ Leveling System.

MAGIC TREE HOUSE®

#2 THE KNIGHT AT DAWN

BY MARY POPE OSBORNE
ILLUSTRATED BY SAL MURDOCCA

A STEPPING STONE BOOK™

Random House 🏠 New York

Magic Tree House®

#1: Dinosaurs Before Dark

#2: The Knight at Dawn

#3: Mummies in the Morning

#4: Pirates Past Noon

#5: Night of the Ninjas

#6: Afternoon on the Amazon

#7: Sunset of the Sabertooth

#8: Midnight on the Moon

#9: Dolphins at Daybreak

#10: Ghost Town at Sundown

#11: Lions at Lunchtime

#12: Polar Bears Past Bedtime

#13: Vacation Under the Volcano

#14: Day of the Dragon King

#15: Viking Ships at Sunrise

#16: Hour of the Olympics

#17: Tonight on the *Titanic*

#18: Buffalo Before Breakfast

#19: Tigers at Twilight

#20: Dingoes at Dinnertime

#21: Civil War on Sunday

#22: Revolutionary War on Wednesday

#23: Twister on Tuesday

#24: Earthquake in the Early Morning

#25: Stage Fright on a Summer Night

#26: Good Morning, Gorillas

#27: Thanksgiving on Thursday

#28: High Tide in Hawaii

For a list of Magic Tree House® Merlin Missions and other Magic Tree House® titles, visit MagicTreeHouse.com.

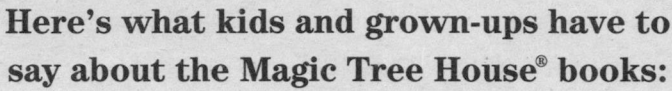

Here's what kids and grown-ups have to say about the Magic Tree House® books:

"Oh, man . . . the Magic Tree House series is really exciting!"
—Christina

"I like the Magic Tree House series. I stay up all night reading them. Even on school nights!"
—Peter

"Jack and Annie have opened a door to a world of literacy that I know will continue throughout the lives of my students."
—Deborah H.

"As a librarian, I have seen many happy young readers coming into the library to check out the next Magic Tree House book in the series."
—Lynne H.